THE POET SPEAKS

THE CAUSE IS THE POET SPEAKING TO ALL

Clifton Sanders

authorHOUSE

AuthorHouse™
1663 Liberty Drive
Bloomington, IN 47403
www.authorhouse.com
Phone: 1-800-839-8640

First published by AuthorHouse   7/29/2009

ISBN: 978-1-4490-0136-0 (sc)

Printed in the United States of America
Bloomington, Indiana

This book is printed on acid-free paper.

HEY! WE CAN'T GET IT BACK

Let us accelerate time to appreciate the moment
 because when the moment is wrong, the moment is gone.
 Emptiness in the place of amazement
 gives the heart a weak contentment.
 In fact,
I am waiting on you
 while you are longing for me.
 We cannot go back to a future
 that never had a past
 and the reality of a lack of romance in our past is yet to be considered.
 The love we never made,
and all the joy in our hearts,
 we never saved.
Even the love, peace,
 and happiness that we never gave,
 but so desired the experience.
 It would have been nice to have it all
rolled into one,
so that we could have held it in our hearts,
and waited for one another there.
 Therefore,
 in the future,
 let us learn to wait for the other,
 since *we can't get it back.*
FOOD FOR THOUGHT

BE - CAUSE

Consider our reasons for being blessed and empowered by Christ to clean mess and to lead a cause that meets need. We must give way to needs of sacrifice in the world to exemplify the cause of Christ. Although God is a cause, He is still the great Uncaused Cause. Because we need Jesus to please us in the world today, and we need the power of God to accomplish a destiny that gives to our way. For it takes power to change from a wrong track to a better destiny. To put it bluntly, it is having no other way; otherwise, it would not be so. Not so means no- more of the usual rationale, which entails a reason for the pattern of movement and targets habits while they are in a course of action. Be but for what needs more than the original attention. Span and expand the essence of being more than it can. Whence a being is stretched, thence it joins cause not by fear, just be-cause.

"I HAVE A GENE" HENCE, I LOOK LIKE SOMEBODY!

I have a gene that has to be seen, and through my heredity there is a gene that has never been seen in the spitting image of my off-spring's gene. I have a gene and I look like somebody! I have a gene means that I am an off-spring. In the city of Fort Pierce, Florida, year nineteen hundred and seventy six, my parents suffered from a case of bumpy love; - that is, seed and egg collided, thirty-two years latter, here I come, and I look like somebody. I am the product of bumpy love; my father always claimed me as his offspring, but even if my father never claimed me, I claim his genealogy. It is my genealogy that causes me to notice what I see, but the real me is seen in my heredity. That is, my very appearances reaches out; and sacks my father by the neck and shout " Hey, I look like you! " I have I have a gene that cannot be seen, unless it is seen in my heredity. Heredity is the history of seeing my gene, and I say that one day in my heredity, by the grace of al-mighty God, that even in the year 3,076 you all will still see me looking like somebody.

Now you see me and later will not, so watch out for thence I com LOL! I promise to make a com up in the future. God bless America and remember that you all are never too late for any thing as long as you all are coming. Late when you get there, but coming and some might not get there when I get there, but we are coming back together again and we all look like some body.

Y'ALL DON'T HEAR ME, THOUGH

Subliminal seduction results when actions speak louder than words. Actions can cause a low or a high frequency of attention. Action speaks to, addresses, and triggers attention without words. The average time span for attention is five minutes, and it is given to be intrinsically felt, not heard. So, the proclamation "Y'all don't hear me though" has to be heard to recollect hearing to receive the content of its vernacular in the present tense, but the goal of conversation is to know, and comprehend conversation immediately after it was spoken. Words in conversations, messages, or sermons are often spoken aloud, yet not say anything at the same time. Human nature remembers not words, messages, or great sermons; they receive understanding, then he or she knows, what caused him or her to remember the impression of the spirit, actions, and what was done for him or her. For that reason, without subliminal seduction of the present tense, we cannot hear what we heard.

WHAT DID YOU SAY?

Subliminal seduction is a life - changing experience that is embedded into the nature of human fabric. It is unnoticed by the natural eye; people choose perfect dialogue to execute, hoping to seduce one another without knowing the intent for the reason that we must be brought out of the past tense and into the present tense. They do not know that we cannot grasp, understand, and hear the words without recollection. Our life span issues are roles to be developed, and roles have their parts, but as a result, our role play are developed into our roles in society, which is through the learning of parts that we develop and play, which is symbolic to filling a job vacancy. What subliminal messages rather than actions are being transmitted to students in the education system?

MISGUIDED YOUTH

As an ex- ESE paraprofessional special education teacher, sometimes I felt stretched and expanded, but I saw young lives developed. I taught middle school, which is where most are face-to-face with puberty, adolescence, hormones, peer pressure, and development in their bodies. The students looked like little people, and this is a critical time in their lives, because if they were without recollection, this means they would not know how to do their class - works in middle school. To improvise, when students are put in the next grade without meeting the requirements, those student are being set up for failure; because there are testes given to attain a diploma, and basic life skills are learned in middle school. I took a high school graduation test to receive my diploma based on the understanding I learned in middle school. In other words, my high school diploma was issued to me in middle school. Sadly to say that a lot of the students did not take education seriously because some of the students were failing; I admonished them to simply take the test, but they were without fear of what would become of them without education, so they did not hear what I had to say.

ACTIONS SPEAKS LOUDER THAN WORDS

When the focus is more on disciplining rude students, and on unruly actions rather than on the assignment; students got in trouble, and really did not know what they did or why they got in trouble; their only explanation was they acted bad. When I asked them what caused them to act badly; I would get a hundred different explanations because words are dense when it is attention people want. We should never let it be said that our actions do not speak for what we say because we ought to mean what we say and say what we do. Since our actions, services, nature, and impression will always constitute and compliment our words, subliminal seduction is not how extensive or elegant that we live, but significance is in the life that we live because people understand people, who leave impression; otherwise, without subliminal seduction of the past tense, we cannot hear the heard.

THE OBJECTIVE OF EMPTINESS

Nature is objective when needs resides inside neglected. That which needed is up most miss-leaded and dip leaded in origin. The original transcript void of blueprint is issue to fulfillment. Danger is when miss of kiss coincides with others alluring gist to his/her best wish. Thus, the emptiness of void cause hate among some who help those emptied. Nature is maker and objective is perceptive; yet projective upon the scene of intention verses means.

Faulty intentions make the soul sank to low dimensions. Hence, trapped in low life spent too much time in happened since. Thus, great happenings of emptiness are present tense. Thence, loneliness is a disease that infuses a disk-ease. Like a plea of help swept under the sleep of the world that see he/her normally. The heart beats a creep or a beast turned monster to least expected. When individuals find emptiness, they cannot help it, but fall victim to the track of emptiness in them.

I TAKE FIND IN YOU

Find however goes deeper than the ocean,
 wider than the sea,
 even larger than the behind.
  In fact, all that I lost,
 I left it behind that I may find.
  So I know that it is a fine,
 baby rocking my mine because I can't find,
 but still until I find,
 I take find in you.

I HEAR THE SOUND

I hear the sound of a mighty rushing wind,
 even before it begins.
 I can hear the sound of when
 while it gains.
 I hear the sound of a powerful winning,
and it is stronger now than it ever has been.
  There is a sound of win from beginning to end in the midst of happenings
 and a battle cry of praises sound like it over and over again.
 There is a sound of ended and ponder felt with bliss and wonder.
 The gracious sound that my ear cannot hear but
 my vision is clear.
For the very rejections of life are the sound waves of Christ.
When God gives sounds,
 let all else cease for sake of the wave.
 There is a wave and when we get into the wave,
 we get into what He has made
 and it sounds good.
  In fact,
 feel the wave of sound.
 Hear the wave of sound at the time you are rushing it
 because we ride the wave of life to take us to a place in Christ.
So let us get into the wave by hearing the sound.

THE BLACK EYE EFFECT

The nature of receiving a black eye happens by cause and effect,
and all that is affected by pressure
and force of the punch
alters the face's appearance by noticeable recognition
that makes a difference to the person,
as opposed to the face itself.
A black eye is ineffective without a cause,
and change is not noticed without its difference.
I use the analogy of a black eye to note differences in my city,
the City of Fort Pierce, Florida.
The effects of a black eye on my city are changing everything in it
Because of the differences
Change changes change because there was a need for change;
change changed my city;
and when the city changed, I changed.

CHANGE CHANGES CHANGE

Just as a lion hunting on his prowl of destiny,
I used critical thinking as my prey
to decide to change my career because my situation changed.
So, I changed my whole perspective about my education.
No longer do I satisfy myself with past accomplishments.
My best goals are in the past,
and I cannot change with a city advancing for the better
without shifting myself.

HE PUNCHED ME IN THE FACE

God gave me a black eye
 because it was hard for me to change my mind
about leaving the school board,
 and furthering my education.
 He punched me in the face,
 and swelling did not take place until I made a conscious decision
to change for the reason that I did not realize that my face had already changed.
 Although,
the land is not the man,
my face is the place.
In this place,
I could not get a job with the education I had.
I got mad when I worked a month each for two jobs;
unfortunately,
I was unable to qualify for Medicaid
because I had not enough work made to afford a bandage .
Other jobs required a master's degree to work with youth,
 and to tell you the truth,
no master's degree meant no work for me.
 To each his own,
 to own his place,
God meant it for good,
 but I felt like He punched me in the face.

ROLL CALL

After a struggle to finally accomplish a goal,
we need to reach it by being present for roll call.
 Roll call in us becomes presence
and responsibility out of us.
 For it means that we are here;
 and we can never show up here
or present for roll call at work
 if we never been there.
 Consequently, the happenings of life
 takes us there, where, and back,
and we answer the presence of the call.
So, every job has to answer to its call.
We were created for a roll or purpose
that calls personality to fulfill attendance, and compliment the knowledge of any position.

BEWARE OF THE UNKNOWN KNOWN

Is it not wrong to be unknown?
 as long as awareness is gone.
 We really don't miss the unknown
until its gone.
 There was a popular song,
 " The Thrill Is Gone."
 The thrill in awareness see
 is no mystery.
 It is exposed
like a boy acting bad
with a booger in his nose
and does not know of his awareness to bear witness
 with his forgetfulness
 to blow his nose.

THE REAPER

Mr. Reaper may the good Lord keep yah
 consumed with life in Christ;
 No jive because you take life; take it live and
reap God's sacrifice of eternal life to the full

I NEEEED THEE OHHHH

We do not want God until we need God, and we do not really need God until we trust God to come to know and experience Him. So, usually it is no plead form we without our need of He. Savior is our battle cry for not to pass us by. Whine on others Thy are calling, nigh why must we deny the most high a piece of our sky.   We negate the safe and wait the late when the going is tough and times are to put our trust in God, and we do not trust unless it is by force or no other choice in the hour of situation; or a burst of frustration and meager reaction. Like Mick Jaggier said, "I Can't Get No Satisfaction."

MAY THE SHOE FIT WHO PUTS IT ON

You are not hurt as much as you are confronted
 and made to be held accountable for the lie you told.
Just like a virgin kissed for the very first time,
I long to debate with you in accuracy.
 I do not say much on purpose,
 But I listen to everything with a purpose,
 and everything you have is equivalent to a lie.
 The truth of the matter is we were all brainstorming
and Isabal went out of town.
 I presented my case study
 and asked you what do you think
 and waited for a reply.
 When Isabal went out of town,
 you replied back to me
with approval of my case study.
 You even assigned parts to the team assignment.
This matter is not one of right and wrong,
It is a matter of who puts on any offense.
Consequently,
your claims went through interrogation,
and found to be the wrong fit for me;
 Due to accuracy,
however,
I never!
Further alignment to the truth of this matter
 occurred when Isabal got back in town,
and took your authority,
 and made you a liar.
 Therefore,
 may the shoe fits,
 and shove it up you nose.

MR BIG STUFF

Having good faith is equivalent to possessing
 the very substance or stuff of **things** hoped for,
 is equivalent to having the evidence of the substance of things not seen.
 To receive faith is not to receive things,
 because things are made of substance
 and substance makes up things,
 so we need to receive the stuff that made the things possible.
 Once again,
 good faith possesses what we already have,
and not things we want,
 when it is faith's stuff
that we need ownership of.
 Therefore,
 it is no backing away from anything;
 when I have stuff that makes things change.
Even though I am small in things,
I am big in stuff;
and for that reason
I have more stuff than things;
 I am your Mr. Big Stuff.

WHO DO YOU THINK YOU ARE!

Many times, we have the ability without the capacity, but we have the potential to be gigantic and no power to grasp potential to hold greatness. Because we are not what we do in order to be who we are, even though we are who we think we are in spite of what we do; in essence, if one thinks he can, then he can and if he thinks he cannot then he cannot.

SEEING IS BELIEVING

We comprehend what we perceive, perceive what we see, and see what we experience, and we learn from the experience, in addition to knowing what we learned from to compliment what we saw.

WORK THAT THING

Applicability is the act of being able to apply that stuff, savvy or know how. No one may have equal abilities; however, we all have a measure of stuff, equal to our ability to work our stuff by mixing it with the substances of all things desired or hope for.

PULLERS

Pullers bring out the best in us, by our simply seeing the best in them, so just as a preacher pulls behind a pull pit, so do pullers influence the character of friends and individuals. Therefore, we need friendships with individuals who we admire because they reached the goals that we aspire. Just by encouraging me is a pull from he who pulls to the same degree of accessory. Thus pullers.

THIS IS WHO I AM

Born tenth of thirteen siblings,
I am a thirty three year old African American native of Fort Pierce, Florida.
When challenging goals are set before me,
I crave the result of what could become of my future
if I do not give up on my goals.
When I was overcoming a near fatal car accident
while attending the Indian River Community College
with only fifteen credits,
who could have known
that it would lead to sixty credits
with an associate of arts in history.
Who would have known
that an associate of arts degree was not the end result?
I transferred to Palm Beach Atlantic University
and graduated with a bachelor
of arts in Christian Leadership.
I wanted to attend Palm Beach Atlantic University
because of its Christian emphasis on education.
When God saved me from that near fatal car accident,
my recovery was extensive,
but quick.
I stayed in a coma for a month and a half,
but by God's grace,
I relearned how to walk,
talk,
eat,
read
and write.
In five months,
I was back home
with a traumatic brain injury,
that caused epilepsy
and seizures.
The car accident could have resulted in death,
but impending death was the catalyst

God used to awaken me to self worth
and purpose;
although the accolades,
 goals
 and achievements were nice,
 they now facilitated the purpose and meaning of my life.
there is a greater meaning for life,
 and it is not that I was on the dean's list or received accolades
or degrees.
 These degrees do not define who I am;
they simply take me to another level.
When I find purpose
 I find life;
 with out life
 I do not know who I am,
 but I am content with becoming who I am.

CAN

First, we do what we "can", and the intrinsic belief that someone "can" denotes the ability to unlock potential and   may result in an action that helps to define identity.   Identity is the outcome of the interplay between unseen actions yet to happen in the future and who we are at the moment.

TAKE A LOOK AT ME NOW!

Some of us look good looking, so the saying, "Hey good looking, what's you got cooking" makes clear that a person's present state looks better or has been changed to be better looking. Then, there are some exposed as looking for the past attention in the present dimension. They are left looking for things that they never found before they started looking and cooking. Consequently, in this poem, looking has close ties to cooking. Evidently, the past cooked, and the presence looks at us now. The word " take " in the English vernacular is a word of exchange; so when I take, you take or you take I take. In addition, the word take means that some one can take some thing without giving some thing in return. Looking and jucking and even at times tooking in the face of what one could have. Precious memories made sad because the past is the only way to catch your rabbit tat ash. Make no mistake when I take, you take. Because I have taken time to address you, look at me now.

ALL THINGS AT WORK FOR ME

Even with no things, all things are at work, for me. Even when it may appear that all things are at work against me, faith takes one into a dimensions, eyes cannot see. There is no such thing as blind faith because faiths see like a referee. Therefore, in the plight of no things, I rejoice in all things that are restored in the great happenings for me. Just as if a farmer with seeded field knows that all things are working for his happening that was not bought into the seeing. A great happening is interchangeably used to relate to the being. Therefore, the words happen being constitutes for what one happens to see all around.

DELIGHT YOUR SELF IN IT

We need to learn to benefit it only if we would delight our selves in it. Success best are expressed in times spent with no request. For the Bible declares of a promise that bears with the delightment that birthed unexcitment rather an unwanted need to read and study hard. However, when the going gets tough, easy is hard, and hard is as good. For the mind to recline is sign of interest to an attention feast. It is responsibility upon us to study and bring light in order to sight the inner working of heart. Where our drives are, drives for us to become. God's desire is to make one into a desire. To put it bluntly, the reveal to learning is to a learned in a learning that we are the blessing. Liking to a hospital, we are a caregiver to deliver, who been made by the challenges in it our enjoyment in it. We learn to progress in times of peace with no stress and we need only benefit if we learned to get in it.

TAKE NO "BS"

It is nice to know that there is a common unity concerning BS, that is, we take none of it! If our BS stands for some - thing, it would never fall for any - thing. When we take no BS, we spread and give away a lot of our BS. Therefore, not taking is the same as giving and making Consequently, it is a give and take to BS because many times we give it and take it, break it and even forsake it. To put it bluntly, we do not take it because we are too busy giving it away. We are what we believe, and we do what we believe. As a Christian, I have a BS or belief system that I hold very dear to my heart, because Jesus died for it, the Spirit maintains it, and God demands it. We have to believe in order to receive likeness and nature, which is not of ourselves, but we develop personality by our dealings with one another.

RAGE LIKE A SHOTGUN

My father, under the influence of alcohol was as a trigger pulled; A consequence of my father's rage is the result of my twelve -- gauge rage, per se. Twelve-gauge rage is kind of far – fetching the truth, one catches impact of the father's nature in the next generation representing the seed or children of the father. Therefore, when my father displayed rage, anger, and madness in front of me, he shot the same anger, and madness into me; he shot the same anger and madness into me in the form of me in the form of fear. In essence, far – fetching can be used In essence, far – fetching can be used in the analogy of playing with an explosive bomb, by which the father passes explosives to his family and it comes back up in their natures during fearful situations.

I WENT BUNKERS

My personality is of a quiet, good, well-mannered, Christian nature, mainly because I do not want to resemble my father's alcoholic, abusive nature, and some how discover that fruit does not fall far from the tree. For example, in 2002, I moved to Atlanta, and roomed with a friend; I was unemployed because of a recession. My roommate pressured me and gave me a deadline to find employment; my friend gathered with his other friends, and made fun of my failed attempts to find employment. He stated how I needed him, and I did because he provided for my room and board. Eventually, my friend told me to get out of his apartment in a mean tone of voice. I always did the cooking in my roommate's apartment since my parents taught me how to cook because I always cooked for my self. He told me that it was my fault that I was not working; so I contributed to him while I stayed in his apartment by cleaning the house, washing the laundry, and cooking the meals that I bought with my food stamp card. And to clarify, yes I continued to contribute by cooking, cleaning , and doing laundry because I was new to Atlanta, and I had no other place to go. To suffer is to endure willingly and I did suffer because I knew that God saw me and was going eventually change my situation. Therefore, I did not freely go back home, in essence, I took abuse in the way that a battered wife would from an abusive husband.

However, when my roommate threatened me with an eviction from his apartment onto the Atlanta streets; I totally lost it because it represented the same childhood experience I had with my father. My father would come home drunk and scream at the top of his lungs, "I hate the ground you walk on;" He would then beat my family, starting with my mother. During the beating from a three –hundred- pound, profanity speaking mad man, whom I thought was going to kill my mother and older siblings. Because I was considered one of my mother's babies, she placed me and three more of my younger siblings in our back room under the bed. She ordered us to stay in the back room with the door locked. Me and my younger siblings were scared for my mother and older sibling so we started praying in tears. We were so scared that we hid under the bed and hoped the abuse taking place was a bad dream hoping my father would stop hurting my mother and older siblings. Like wise, I started screaming at my roommate and his friends, "I hate you "at the top of my lungs and jumped around screaming, tearing food out the boxes, and dumping it on the floor. Once I calmed down, God revealed to me that my fathers rage was not my rage, but the fear of rage is in me. Given the right environment, atmosphere, and situation, I was a time bomb waiting to go off.

My family and social relationships were formed in my mother's ability to hold my family together with prayer, and by believing in a higher power to bless her children. It is important to note, I believe that some of the most abused and battered families are some of the closest families. This past ordeal of alcoholic abuse by my father made us closer, but it also raised differences in my heart between my siblings and my self because I felt that my older siblings could have bettered themselves in spite of my father's abusive addiction to alcohol. I experienced a near fatal car accident and stayed in a coma for a month and a half. I had to relearn to walk, talk, read and write and I am   where I am in my life today only by the grace of God. My accident was one of the best things that ever happened to me; because despite all the sadness and tragedy, God found me, and I will never be the same. In fact, I have a backbone of my own because God has given me value and a purpose for existing.

SOMEBODY NO ONE KNOWS

I thought that my older siblings were smarter than me, and some really were. I wanted to be just like my brothers' and sisters' because I did not like who I was. In essence, I had a void in my heart that my brothers and sisters could not fill. Undoubtedly, my main characteristic was being the brother of my brothers and sisters; people knew me because of who I was connected to. As a result, I felt like somebody's relative whom nobody knew. I wore other people's values as my values and hid behind the values of other people in my family.

IT'S A GET TO!

 No, people do not have a right to die because it's a get to; life is not a have to, it is a get to, and the rich cannot pay their way out of it. As a Christian, I do not have to pay my tithes, I get to pay my tithes. It was said that the only rights a person has is to eat sleep and die, and with out these rights, one does not need a legal contract to die.   . I believe that the human race did not create themselves; they have no right to buy the right with assistance, which is really a death certificate to kill them. Although, individuals my buy a right to kill themselves, it is not right for the rich to buy a certificate to kill themselves. Even though, a person is free to commit suicide, but with assistance, it is a homicide. I strongly believe that only the creator of life has the right to take a life, and all other reasons are a copout request of the fortunate. WHY, I believe that only the wealthy think they could buy their way out of pain and suffering. Poor people do not want to get to suffer, but they have to suffer, and when they had suffered long enough, they get to die because God sees fit to calls them home. Technically speaking, God does not cause any one to suffer and die, but we cause our selves to suffer and die with foods we eat, lifestyle we live, and we have the audacity to blame it on God when He do not heal us from choices we made in the past. In fact, none of life is a have to because we get whatever we make out of it.

Research Methodology Paper:
Concepts of psychology
Clifton T. Sanders
University of Phoenix Online
PSYCH 535 Multicultural Psychology
Katia Araujo, Psy. D.
January 28, 2009

ABSTRACT

According to the text, many observers (e.g., Dumont, 1983) have cited Protestantism as a shadow of individualism. Thus, various Francophone scholars have long discussed the concept of individualism as characteristic of Western peoples; a recent example is in the work of Cohen-Emerique (1991). The role values play in a tradition is a distinction between levels of analysis. Hence, levels of analysis in society give everyone in it the same importance. Whereas, same as the text, enculturation and socialization are sources of influence from within a tradition; that is useful to examine sampled aspects of culture by sampling the current and historical population change that came about as a result of internal forces. The samples are like observations since, interaction between cultures determined the sociopolitical context therefore, their interactions are those that determine the population context, which, of course, interact with both the ecological context and with the process variables. Inspiring conformity and hard work, to the rules, all in the hope of "making it," with some actually doing so.

Research Methodology Paper

According to the text, many observers (e.g., Dumont, 1983) have cited Protestantism as a shadow of individualism. Thus, various Francophone scholars have long discussed the concept of individualism as characteristic of Western peoples; a recent example is in the work of Cohen-Emerique (1991). In contrast, to traditional and multicultural research on Western philosophies, religious and political ideologies have been pointed at least by the sources of collectivism (Segall – et al. 1999, p. 209).

In observation and sampling, there are many similarities and differences in reference to traditional and multicultural research. The role values play in a tradition is a distinction between levels of analysis. Hence, levels of analysis in society give everyone in it the same importance. For instance, the process of acculturation is a sociopolitical and historical context or tradition within a culture. Hence, this process parallels cultural transmission from the inside that affects the outside. Segall et al. (1999) reported:

> A second line of argument was introduced in Chapter 2 in a preliminary description of the ecocultural framework: The sociopolitical and historical context of a group also potentially influences the development and display of human behavior, through the process of acculturation. This process parallels that of cultural transmission, which was described earlier as comprising the dual phenomena of enculturation and socialization. In the case of acculturation, the sociopolitical context influences the individual from outside one's own culture, whereas enculturation and socialization are sources of influence from within one's culture (Acculturation, p. 299).

Whereas, same as the text, enculturation and socialization are sources of influence from within a tradition; that is useful to examine sampled aspects of culture by sampling the current and historical population change that come about as a result of internal forces. Thus, some of those forces are samples, such as social innovation and invention, and population explosion in a society. All of these factors are likely to contribute to social instability, at times leading to social change, which in turn requires individuals to then adapt psychologically. Winderowd, Montgomery, Stumblingbear, Harless, and Hicks (1987) reported:

> Enculturation is an important construct in understanding the traditional cultural experiences of American Indian/Alaska Native (AI/AN) people. Whereas *acculturation* has been defined as "the degree to which the individual … accepts and adheres to both majority (White/Euro-American) and tribal cultural values" (Choney, Berryhill-Paapke, & Robbins, 1995, p. 76), *enculturation* is the process by which an individual learns about and identifi es with his or her own cultural roots (Little Soldier, 1985; Whitbeck, Chen, Hoyt, & Adams, 2004; Zimmerman, Ramirez, Washienko, Walter, & Dyer, 1994). *Traditionality* (Solomon, Arugula, & Gottlieb, 1999) is another term used in the literature to denote enculturation and is similarly thought to be an adherence to cultural values and behaviors that define an AI/AN perspective or way of life (Sanders, 1987, p. 1).

The samples are like observations since interaction between cultures determined the sociopolitical context therefore, their interactions are those that determine the population context, which, of course, interact with both the ecological context and with the process variables. According to the text, observation denotes comparisons that constitute contrast between individualistic and collectivistic societies.   For the reason that samples and observations are component and compliment each other. Dasen et al. (1999) reported:

> In much research, comparisons of samples of people in the United States and Japan are treated as if these comparisons constitute contrasts between individualistic and collectivistic societies, and obtained differences in the selected behavior are then sometimes attributed to individualism/collectivism, as if they were "causes" of the obtained differences. We shall make clear later in this chapter that we deplore this practice because it epitomizes circular reasoning (Beliefs, Motives and Values, 208).

Observation and sampling are different with multicultural and traditional methods because they are quite confusing like individualism and collectivism working together. For example, traditional methods versus individualism / collectivism are metaphors. Poortingo et al. (1999) stated:

> There is nothing about how either of the two "national cultures" might impact. There is seldom even a discussion, fanciful or otherwise, about how the alleged individualism of one society and the alleged collectivism of the other might shape students in the putatively more collectivistic culture differently from their counterparts in the putatively more individualistic one (Beliefs, Motives, and Values p. 217).

Some times in a multicultural society it may seem to be a mockery of a group of people because their values are encouraged by an elite group in their society, fostered at the verbal level; when in fact they hardly exist, specifically the mass media.   Inspiring conformity and hard work, to the rules, all in the hope of "making it," with some actually doing so. Cardon (19995) made mention:

> The research is unique in that it measures four types of the I-C dimension: horizontal individualism, vertical individualism, horizontal collectivism, and vertical collectivism, as conceptuahzed by Triandis (1995). Furthermore, it emerges from the premise that cultures are neither strictly collectivist nor individualist; rather, cultures have profiles in which individualist tendencies are prominent in some circumstances whereas collectivist tendencies are emphasized in others (Horizontal and Vertical Individualism and Collectivism, p 2).

> The horizontal measure of collectivism is measured by individualism in societies. In the same way, samples are the measure of observation. Whereas, enculturation and socialization are measures of tradition. Therefore, in this study of multicultural, the psychologist needs to sample and observe societies to reference traditions through society.

References

Berry, J., W. Dasen, P., R.. Poortinga, Y., H. Segall, M., H. (1999). Human behavior in global perspective: An introduction to cross – cultural psychology (2nd ed.). Needham Heights, 208, 217. MA: Allyn & Bacon / Pearson.

Harless, D. Hicks, K. Montgomery, D. Stumblingbear, G. and Winderowd, C. (2008). American Indian and Alaska Native Mental Health Research. The Journal of the National Center, 15 (2) 1 – 14, 2. Retrieved January 30, 2009 from EBSCOhost Data Base.

SO FALL ON YOUR KNEES

When God is speaking, it is a cease from yeast because they fall to their knees.' Please, there must be ease with God and not the hard that stop the channel of God, for the channel makes known the span of God. Therefore, if one is trying to sleep and cannot, maybe God is trying to say something. Our only immunity is to come into the unity and be found because all else distractions are leasers spans and be at cease to be at peace with God. Although God is in the cease, He is not decease from keeping His peace. Consequently, the peace of God is His span and all of creation has been given a span to appease the ease of God. Prayer gives God an undivided attention span that is why the average attention span for man is five minutes. All other spans are enemies' of God, so He makes them hard on purpose to convince us. We must under stand that God lives in stillness, dwells in quietness, and reveals Himself in a hush. Hence, let me therefore, hush, and be at peace to come into the unity before I fall on my knees.

FIGHT THE FEEL

We fight the feel to know the real release from a thrill of a sense to enter that, which is meant. Still, the will must be honest like a bowl for its meal. Hence, we must conquer however, we feel to live in thrill and feel the freedom of His will. For reason that I feel like I feel to know that His joy set before me is real. Thus, the feeling is infilling and whence we start living, we fight to enter the true dimension of the feel.

AND THEY ALL FELL DOWN

There is yeast that must decrease in quake of release. We go-through to get thrown, and when through, we are through so boo-hoo. Besides, they all fell down to the ground, get down whence arise and enemies' are made to scatter. No matter or substance to whence the great author is penning. Who so ever, will never, so take fate and demonstrate the will of Kill Bill, hence. No thrill its gone, if not loving is right, thence do not want to be wrong. Too grown for too long in this Genesis, so go forth and finish this, Ring around the town, and they all fell down. The very best of falling is the getting, for we get to get back up again. Hence, the secret to again is one more gain, and the secret in getting up is making up again; but first things first and they all fell down.

THE YOUNG AND THE RESTLESS

When Cyndi Lauper recorded her 1983 hit; "Girls Just Want to Have Fun," it made a clear bias in genders, but a certainty in ambiguity. For boys just want something to do with the fun they could have. The reality of just wanting something to do with just having fun is mysterious. Consequently, young girls just want fun and are unwilling to wait on the young boys to mature; The young boys just need to find a cover to stay out of trouble. While the girls are delighting in sighting, young boys are too busy fighting in bad tidings. Indeed, the skirt viruses the hurt comprised is hurting the skirt. Lessons are learnedt, but rarely tested, when both are seeking what they just need, young and restless.

TIME LANGUAGE: TIME WILL TELL

The act of being out of step with the past dispensation of one's reality is the same as being thrust into further actuality in space, time, and contingency. Time has no secrets' because over time will tell, in fact, it is only a matter of time to wait for its tell, hence, time tell. Ever heard of timetables? Well, time will tell on the table in a matter of time. Matter is a thing and every thing has its wait that speaks through the events of the occurrences'- that happen, and not events that did not happened, therefore, it does not matter because it did not happen.

NATURE CALL

Squaring never to be like any thing is impossible, for it is a power from the normal ordinariness of life, we are like the first impression of somebody's nature, and time after there is a call. It was said that deep call unto deep, but nature calls unto its own as well, and we have been begotten of natural ordinariness of life because we have been begotten of natural forces and causes. Hence, the human's being has a nature seen in conduct and construct.

FOR HERE OR THE GO?

Give me that go is the reason for coming to a sense of a higher power, so with power invested go get them to come. Passion and annuity in using the old pro come nigh Jesus, here I go. I know no mountain high enough, valley low. Say no more, I am as a whore for life to make known the forgiveness in Christ. For here or the go; I be your go-getter for life for Christ with a changed life. There I went, but here I go like a whore to show-go the logo that I must go. Too slow so catch me here, but I rather go. Whence zero hence no more thence hero thus must go!

TIMBER ME WHISKERS

To the pedigree of the analogy timber me suggest a measure of flattery done to get her, and her whiskers is her whisper. Yet, it does not excuse her wooden nature, which is another part of attitude regardless of stature. The ability to have stats with no score makes stature a pigmentations or aggravations as well of the imagination, when she is merely shaking what her mama gave her. As a result, her force field is she is real. It is like taking the thrill out of reveal only to reveal another will cannot conceal the sight in her out to give. Keep it real, kill Bill not Jill, and you might get with her only if you timber her whisker.

A PSYCHOPATHIC HOLD TO CONTROL

When a house is not a home due to conditions in the environment, it is psychopathic in nature Because the line does not align with its design, per se. Most criminals are repeat offenders due to lack of understanding that their environment is not everlasting, but is related to psychopathic feedback in their framework of reactions that is seen as lasting in behavior each time the reactions are repeated. Consequently, if these reactions to conditions in the surroundings, atmosphere, setting, and population are not corrected, the outcome in the inhabitation is psychopathic.

Patterns are formed in recurring actions that condition some over a period of time; and these patterns take most out of their dispensation into another situation due to a lack of constraint and control over their intellectual capacity. Similarly, a pattern of control or conditions causes criminals to repeat crime, and as a result, return to imprisonment repeatedly. With out a doubt, a psychopathic checklist revised for criminals is an instrument that will condition criminals to conditions in an environment out side of incarceration.

ROCK AND ROLL

Like a rock that threatens to roll control over, even the souls that tarry in the valley smashing every desire and care. To make Himself known, He has to rock worlds and leave them in total dismay, binding Himself to the only way to fix what brought the result to doom in the day. It is no other way, but the straight way, Holy Ghost say He allowed the rock to drop, but it do not stop. Holy Ghost move, roll, and brood over to find, discover, and cover even the faintest soul. Therefore, on the plight of my misery, please remember to rock, Holy Ghost, roll over to cover, even me.

ITS ON !

The wait is over and time has begun. Shake, let the earth tremble at the tarry of His raft and the wait forsaken. Make rerun to the song and enter the play, and a death be allotted to restriction. The ambiance is set ablaze, a permission due to incision. Like the song, "We Only Just Begun." So, when the clouds be low and shade made so I know the sigh of the cry and the moan of groan at its infancy and a longing made be. It is a bliss wish to do this and it won't be long because it is already on. In the atmosphere, bear with the chemosphere of the loud and clear. The cause has been sparked to unlock the clock of our time to be sprung and every hindrance made rung. The sense_ "Let's_" just do this is in the atmosphere, and a spark has united a cause. It is on like a pot of neck bones that is already done. The best not over because it only just begun to run the fresh awareness of urgency to act upon. Pause and rewind for deaf ears waiting for my song to be known when it is on, thus, once again its on.

THE ULTIMATE PLEASURE

In the presence of the Lord, there is the fullness of joy, which eliminates want. In essence, God is our fullness, and all things reside in Him, including God. Therefore, it is not a want for any thing, but we seek all things in God. The Christian does not seek life in God because they already have it. Christians are to seek life and life more abundantly. Thence, the ultimate pleasure is life lived more abundantly because God makes Himself our own so that we can have God with us at all times. Because, God has given us Himself a shepherd; we have every moment to enjoy and to fall in love repeatedly and repeatedly, even with good bad and ugly. For that reason falling in love with Jesus is loving the moment. Consequently, when the moment is wrong, the moment is wrong. Still, the ultimate pleasure made is manifest when love is made or given with the entire mind, body and soul. Christians are commanded love God with their mind, body and soul, but they cannot until they love one another. Therefore, the ultimate pleasure is daily interaction with any one . To put it bluntly, the ultimate pleasure demonstrated is in our daily love and concern that we have for one another.

TRUE COLOR IN

There is a true stare of a coloring book,
and it is exposed to the look.
A true view of who, exposed for scrutiny,
So do not take fear of real scenery that prefects' its clearest meaning.
 so please do not be afraid.
 Some of the best of us look like the worst of us,
 and God sees and know all.
For some or maybe many their
Best looks are likened to a coloring book,
and we need not fear of anything,
 so why be afraid to make known the made.
 Still,
 a coloring book gets its look
by the spaces colored in
 that arrests outlook to a broader look
 and that covers all areas of the book.
 A coloring book expands a look
 because it makes one look to fill in the coloring.
 Interesting,
an idea is perfect in the mind,
 but when it put forth actuality thoughts are faults.
 The coloring in get their best fills in kindergartens
 amongst toddlers who care not for faces,
 but have ideas about colors.

THE POET SPEAKS

Some things cannot be stated, expounded upon declared or simply addressed, but some things give way to experience, and knowledge falls subject to expression. In fact, words of phase are ways of the wade that ease tension with intention. However, mess must be addressed to confess the heart of the mind unrestricted and the poet cries out in the way of Cain and Able. The situation speaking for the cause is the poet speaking to all. Our reflections are in our lessons, and the poet speaks to address the mess. Only in response, does the poet speaks to bring correction to reflection of out-come for the teachable, so one need only listen to the poet when he speaks to us. Hence, the poet speaks. His agendas must be our keep and all else cease when the Poet speaks. Important to note, when the poet speaks, listen to the heard to manifest His said because when one word is heard, it is clear that we hear what was said. Although, the preacher is always preaching, remember that the poet is not always speaking.

WHAT'S HAPPENING ?

The events in life that seem not to happen are a spiritual sign of what is happening. When we pray for blessings to take action, change must come before it happens. Consequently, many times we desire the rewards of change; but dread its process. There is an ordinary happening as well as a great happening that will not manifest until it happens. Therefore, the great happening is contingent upon merely asking. In other words, because I ask, thus it happens, and if I fell to ask, it happened. However, the happening, we are reacting to are things seen or unseen everlasting. For that reason what happened is everlasting for the asking, and we do not know until it happens.

ATTACHED TO ENVIRONMENT

A person's mentality must be affected for a behavior to form an attachment to its surroundings. When we fall in love, it attaches real people in society, and the same is with the environment: it is a typological attachment because we are attached or confounded to earth all of the time. Therefore, a factor in society that helps development is when man and woman love one another. This is accomplished through brotherly love, and love is a factor in society that develops personality, culture, and society. The act of being abused and loved gives people in society have in consisted behaviors in harmony with situations and not change, since, change changes change, which helps to develop personality in a society. Furthermore, Abraham Maslow's most famous contribution is the hierarchy of needs, and is summarized through a belief system of the humanistic psychology. The premise is behind a basic hierarchy, which state that we are born with certain needs, we cannot continue life and move upward on the hierarchy. The first levels of our psychological needs are our basic needs, such as food, water, sleep, and oxygen, nothing else matters.

A QUICKIE

Like a lighting flash is gas when acceleration is mash. No need to retrieve because quick makes ease. A jerk identifies a jerk and not motion, other than promotion; otherwise, life would not have any gravitational pull. A shifting explains the depth of the fast lull that needed completion. Life is incomplete until there is an on beat step with a destination. In fact, all of God's creations long for the increasing of the later rain to no longer remain the same. However, it is a quickening for the listening that transforms great happenings. Just a quickie in see return, great happening are birthed and profound reactions means new beginnings. Not with a quiver, but a powerful boost that give performance juice and makes no excuse in real time. Twas the joys of life are incomplete without tarrying of such heat that sneaked a peak and made knowing bleak. Thus, a quickening is a quickie in history turned see in order to be.

Hence, the quickening of life are faster gas in contrast to what made beginning last. For reason, life's improvements are benefits to what, exist. Therefore, the joys and desire of honeymoon are quickened when it is time to get busy in replenishing the stars in the heavens. Ultimately, to see what is meant as occupation and masturbation is the frustration of the lubricatione or the quickening of its embrace. Thus, life is a quickie that needs only get busy!

TAKE IT FROM THERE!

Somewhere out there where, yeah if we get here, we can take it from there! Where is there, when it is clear that were over here where, who cares, hence, take if from there! To be taking eradicates making that is conducing to breaking. Many times the cares, of life make us to break us in order to take us where we are in life. When you break dance, one takes a chance of the hard land on back is the crack that takes there to where, hence, meet up and take it from there! Before and after play are the takings of the day. Blonder is such a wonder if not mad where the care is glad. The thrills are excitements and notions are potions when like the devotion. So, when we get there, take it from where it is no fear. Thus, it is the crave of intimacy that highlights in meeting me. Therefore, there is liking unto the stare of where the mind glairs from outside in for a longing to begin. The body makes near here even when the mind is near and unclear of location from being passively taken. Thus, when we, meet, we can take it from there!

ABOUT THE AUTHOR

Clifton T Sanders has a different way of seeing and viewing the realities of life. He uses understanding to cativate his audience. He is a thirty two year old native of Fort Pierce, FL. Shortly after graduating from high school he was in a near fatal car accident. He was in a coma for a month and a half. The doctors and life gave up on him, but for some reason or cause he did not die. For some cause every faulty prediction from the doctors did not happen. For that cause God is a great because in his life, and now there is a greater meaning in life. He feels that the meaning of life has no natural cause, but a purpose and a reaason for it. He is the tenth born of thirteen siblngs, he graduated from West Wood high school in 1995 because of foot ball. He had a foot ball scalorship and was in a near fatal car accident two week before his departure. He was deformed and crippled so he lost his foot ball scholarship and athletic ability. Two years later he had to get his right lung removed due to unknown causes. Because of the car accident, he had/has epilepsy and a traumatic brain injury. At the same time, he enrolled into the Indian River Community College and graduated in 1999 with an AA degree in history.. He tranfered to Palm Beach Atlantic College and earned a Bacherlor of Arts degree in Christian Leadership in 2001. Now he is currently in graduate school with a major in Science Phychology.